MEDUSA

ARIEL SANDERS

Copyright © 2025 by ARIEL SANDERS
All rights reserved.

No part of this book may be reproduced, stored in a retrieval system, or transmitted in any form or by any means—electronic, mechanical, photocopying, recording, or otherwise—without the prior written permission of the publisher, except in the case of brief quotations used in reviews.

This book is intended for entertainment purposes only. While every effort has been made to ensure accuracy, the author and publisher make no representations or warranties regarding the completeness, accuracy, or reliability of the information contained within. The reader assumes full responsibility for their interpretation and application of any content in this book.

Index

Chapter 1 The Excavation	5
Chapter 2 The Mirror Seal	9
Chapter 3 The First Glimpse	13
Chapter 4 Modern Myth	17
Chapter 5 The Survivor	21
Chapter 6 Mirror of Self	25
Chapter 7 Stone Garden	31
Chapter 8 The Rebirth	37
Chapter 9 The Reflection Ritual	41
Chapter 10 Gaze of the Damned	47
Chapter 11 Legacy of the Gorgon	55

SPECIAL BONUS
Want this Bonus Ebook for *free*?

Chapter 1
The Excavation

The summer heat pressed down on the small Greek island of Kythinos like a weighted blanket, causing sweat to trickle down Dr. Sophia Hass's spine as she carefully brushed away another layer of sediment from the cave floor. Despite the protests from her team about the sweltering conditions, she refused to abandon her work. Her reputation for being brilliant but reckless had followed her across three continents, but it was that same determination that had led to her most significant discoveries.

"Dr. Hass," called Marco, her assistant, ducking his head under the low entrance of the cavern. "The villagers are outside again. They're demanding we leave."

Sophia brushed a strand of ginger hair from her face, leaving a streak of dirt across her forehead. "Tell them what I told them yesterday. And the day before that. This is a sanctioned archaeological excavation with full permissions from the Greek government."

Marco shifted uncomfortably. "It's not about permissions. They're saying this place is cursed. That we're disturbing something that should remain buried."

Sophia sat back on her heels, her keen eyes scanning the unusual markings on the cave wall—serpentine patterns that seemed to coil and twist in the uncertain light of their lamps. "Superstition has prevented scientific discovery for centuries. We're here to find truth, not perpetuate myth."

"They specifically mentioned a Gorgon," Marco persisted. "They say this cave was sealed for a reason."

"Perfect," Sophia smiled, her eyes lighting up with excitement rather than fear. "That aligns with my theory that this could be connected to the Gorgon cult. The archaeological community has long debated whether Medusa was purely mythological or based on an actual person or priestess."

Later that afternoon, as the sun began its descent, Sophia's trowel hit something that wasn't stone. A hollow sound reverberated through the cave.

"Everyone!" she called out, excitement making her voice tremble. "I need all hands here, now!"

Within hours, they had uncovered what appeared to be a sealed entrance beneath the cave floor. The stone slab was engraved with images that made some of her team step back in involuntary fear—intricate depictions of a woman with writhing snakes for hair.

Old Dimitri, their local guide who had reluctantly agreed to help them despite his misgivings, made the sign against evil. "Dr. Hass," he whispered, "this is the tomb the stories speak of. My grandmother told me of this place—where the cursed one sleeps. We must reseal it and leave."

Sophia barely heard him. She was already directing the team to prepare to move the slab. "This could be the archaeological find of the decade," she breathed, oblivious to the growing tension among her colleagues. "Perhaps even the century."

As the stone finally shifted, revealing a dark passageway below, a cold breeze—impossible in the summer heat—wafted up from the depths, carrying with it the scent of something ancient and otherworldly. For just a moment, Sophia's scientific certainty wavered. But curiosity quickly overpowered caution, and she directed her headlamp into the darkness.

"Let's see what secrets you've been keeping," she whispered to the void.

None of them noticed the small fissure that formed at the edge of the opening, nor the barely perceptible mist that began to seep through it, coiling like tendrils of serpentine hair into the world above.

Chapter 2
The Mirror Seal

The tomb beneath the cave defied all of Sophia's expectations. Unlike the cramped confines of the cavern above, this chamber stretched wide, its ceiling high enough that their lights couldn't fully illuminate it. The walls were smooth and covered in frescos remarkably preserved despite the centuries—each depicting scenes of a woman's transformation from beauty to horror, her hair becoming a mass of serpents, her eyes becoming weapons.

"This is unprecedented," Sophia whispered, her voice echoing strangely in the chamber. "These images suggest a narrative about Medusa that doesn't align with the classical myths."

In the center of the chamber stood a curious pedestal. Upon it lay what appeared to be fragments of a broken bronze disk—a shield perhaps, but with a strangely reflective interior surface.

"A mirror-shield," Sophia said, carefully lifting one of the fragments. "Like the one Perseus supposedly used to avoid looking directly at Medusa."

Beyond the pedestal, her light revealed something that sent a chill down her spine. A figure, seemingly carved from stone, was frozen in an attitude of terror—arms raised as if to ward off some terrible sight, face contorted in a scream that had been silenced millennia ago.

"It's so lifelike," Marco whispered, moving closer to examine it. "The craftsmanship is extraordinary."

Sophia frowned. Something about the statue troubled her. The clothing and adornments weren't Greek—they appeared to be

Phoenician. And the level of detail was beyond anything she had seen from that period.

"There's something else here," called Elena, their specialist in ancient artifacts, who had moved to examine the far corner of the chamber.

Nestled in an alcove was a stone container, elaborately carved with protective symbols. When they carefully opened it, they found fragments of what appeared to be a heart—a heart made of stone, cracked into pieces.

"What kind of ritual would involve a stone heart?" Marco wondered aloud.

Sophia carefully cataloged the fragments, placing them in a specimen container. "The myths say nothing of Medusa's heart being turned to stone. This suggests a different version of her story entirely."

As she sealed the container, her fingers brushed against one of the larger fragments. For an instant—so brief she would later doubt it had happened at all—she felt a pulse, as if the stone itself were alive.

That night, in her tent, Sophia dreamed. A woman stood before her, beautiful but weeping tears of blood that carved channels down her face. Her lips moved, forming words in a language Sophia didn't recognize yet somehow understood in the logic of dreams.

"You have awakened me," the woman seemed to say. "But are you worthy to know my truth?"

The woman's hair began to move, not with the wind but of its own accord, transforming into writhing serpents that hissed and struck at the air. When she looked up, her eyes were pools of absolute darkness that seemed to pull at Sophia's very essence.

Sophia woke gasping, her heart racing. Outside her tent, the wind had picked up, carrying with it the faint sound of weeping. But when she emerged to investigate, there was only silence and the distant crash of waves against the rocky shore.

She tried to dismiss it as the product of an overactive imagination, fueled by their discoveries and the locals' superstitions. Yet she couldn't shake the feeling that something had changed—that in opening the tomb, they had disturbed more than just ancient remains.

The fragments of the stone heart sat on her makeshift desk, now assembled into an almost complete whole. In the pale light of her lamp, Sophia could have sworn that for just a moment, a dark liquid seeped from the cracks between the pieces, like blood pulsing through veins of stone.

Chapter 3
The First Glimpse

The next morning, Dimitri didn't show up at the dig site. After waiting for an hour, Sophia sent Marco to the village to check on him, while she and the rest of the team continued their meticulous documentation of the tomb.

When Marco returned, his face was ashen. "Dimitri is gone," he reported. "His wife says he never came home last night. The villagers are organizing a search party, but..." He hesitated. "They're saying it's started. That the curse has been awakened."

Sophia tried to maintain her scientific detachment. "People go missing all the time. Let's not jump to supernatural conclusions."

But later that day, when one of their graduate students failed to return from a routine soil sampling trip to the north side of the cave, the atmosphere in the camp shifted from scholarly excitement to creeping unease.

By sunset, both the villagers' search party and their own efforts had yielded nothing. As the team gathered around the fire that evening, theories ranged from practical concerns about treacherous terrain to whispered fears about the curse.

"We should consider postponing further excavation until we locate our missing team members," suggested Dr. Kalman, the senior archaeologist who had initially been skeptical of Sophia's theories but had joined the expedition out of professional curiosity.

"Abandoning our work now would be premature," Sophia argued, though with less conviction than usual. The dream of the weeping woman still lingered at the edges of her consciousness.

Their debate was interrupted by a scream from the path leading back to the cave. Everyone rushed toward the sound, flashlights cutting through the gathering darkness.

What they found stopped them cold. The graduate student, Mira, had returned—or rather, her body had. But what stood on the path was no longer human. She had been transformed into stone, her face frozen in an expression of absolute terror, her arms raised as if trying to shield herself from something unspeakable.

"It's impossible," Dr. Kalman whispered, reaching out to touch the stone surface that had once been living flesh. "Some kind of elaborate prank or—"

"It's just like the figure in the tomb," Elena cut in, her voice shaking. "The exact same posture, the same expression."

The scientific part of Sophia's mind raced through possible explanations—an elaborate hoax, a rare medical condition, an unknown mineral compound in the cave that could cause rapid calcification. But deep down, she knew they were facing something that defied rational explanation.

As the team backed away from the stone figure that had been Mira, Sophia noticed something at the edge of her vision—a blurred silhouette standing among the trees, its outline strangely indistinct except for what seemed to be moving hair, writhing in the still air.

When she turned to look directly at it, there was nothing there. But the impression remained, along with a bone-deep certainty that they were being watched.

That night, they moved their camp farther from the cave, setting up a rotating watch. No one slept well. The sound of the wind seemed to carry whispers, and more than once, Sophia thought she heard the distant sound of hissing, like a nest of disturbed serpents.

At dawn, they made another grim discovery. Another member of their team, Dr. Kalman, had been transformed during his watch. His stone form was found facing the direction of the cave, his expression one of horrified recognition.

Panic swept through the remaining team members. Two of the graduate students announced they were leaving immediately. Elena was on the satellite phone trying to arrange an emergency evacuation.

"We need to understand what's happening," Sophia insisted, even as fear clawed at her throat. "If this is some kind of... phenomenon related to the tomb, we need to document it, study it."

"Study it?" Marco looked at her incredulously. "Sophia, people are dying—or worse than dying. The legends about the Gorgon... they're real. We've awakened something."

Sophia couldn't bring herself to accept it, not fully. But as she looked toward the cave in the distance, she caught another glimpse of the blurred figure, closer now. For just an instant, their eyes seemed to meet across the distance, and Sophia felt a presence brush against her mind—ancient, sorrowful, and filled with a rage that had simmered for millennia.

The legend of Medusa no longer felt like a myth to be deconstructed and analyzed. It felt alive, unfinished—and hungry for something that Sophia was afraid she might be destined to provide.

Chapter 4
Modern Myth

The next morning, only half of their original team remained. The others had fled back to the village, seeking passage off the island. Sophia couldn't blame them, but she couldn't bring herself to leave—not with the mystery of the tomb still unsolved, and not with the growing certainty that she was somehow connected to what was happening.

"We need expert help," she told Marco and Elena, the only two who had stayed. "Not just archaeological expertise. Someone who understands the myths at a deeper level."

Through a series of urgent calls, they managed to contact Dr. Lillian Thorn, a mythologist specializing in Greek legends who had written extensively on the Gorgon myths. By remarkable coincidence—or perhaps something more fateful—Dr. Thorn had been on a neighboring island for a conference and agreed to travel to Kythinos immediately.

When she arrived the next day, Dr. Thorn was not what Sophia had expected. Rather than the stern academic she had imagined, Lillian was a vibrant woman in her sixties with sharp eyes that seemed to see beyond surfaces and a manner that suggested she had been waiting for this call.

"Show me everything," she said without preamble. "Start with the tomb."

Despite the risks, they returned to the cave. The entrance to the tomb remained open, like a wound in the earth. As they descended, Sophia felt a strange sensation—almost like recognition, as if the tomb itself knew she had returned.

Dr. Thorn moved through the chamber with reverence, her fingers tracing the images on the walls, her lips moving silently as if in conversation with the ancient artists who had created them.

"The classical myth of Medusa is a corruption," she finally said. "A political revision designed to justify Perseus's actions and, by extension, the patriarchal overthrow of earlier goddess cults."

She pointed to a sequence of images they had initially overlooked—a beautiful woman in a temple, a male figure forcing himself upon her, a goddess looking on in anger.

"In the earliest versions, Medusa was not born a monster. She was a priestess of Athena who was violated by Poseidon in Athena's temple. Rather than punishing Poseidon, Athena transformed Medusa—supposedly to protect her, to give her the power to ensure no man could harm her again. But the transformation was also a punishment, an exile."

Sophia frowned. "That version of the myth exists in some sources, but what does it have to do with what's happening now? With people turning to stone?"

Dr. Thorn moved to the broken mirror-shield and the fragments of the stone heart that they had carefully placed back in their original positions.

"The myth tells us that when Perseus killed Medusa and took her head, that was the end of her story. But older versions suggest something different." She pointed to a series of symbols carved around the alcove where the stone heart had been found. "This is a binding spell. A containment. The ancient priestesses who followed Medusa's cult knew that her essence could not be truly destroyed. It was scattered but could reform under the right conditions."

Her finger traced a particular sequence of symbols. "This is a prophecy: 'The one who reflects truth shall awaken the cursed queen.'"

"Reflects truth," Sophia repeated, looking at the broken mirror-shield. "The mirror reflects... but it also distorts, depending on its surface."

"Exactly," Dr. Thorn nodded. "Perseus used the reflection to avoid the truth of what he was doing—killing a victim rather than a monster. The mirror both revealed and concealed reality."

She turned to face Sophia directly. "When you discovered the tomb and disturbed the heart, you began a process that the ancient priestesses feared. Medusa is returning—not just her power, but her consciousness, her memory, her rage."

As if to confirm her words, the temperature in the chamber plummeted. In the shadows beyond their lights, something moved—a darkness deeper than the absence of light, a presence that coiled and uncoiled itself like living tendrils.

"She's here now," Dr. Thorn whispered, her academic detachment giving way to a more primal recognition. "She's watching us. Judging whether we're like those who betrayed her."

Sophia felt it too—the weight of an ancient gaze, assessing her intentions, her worthiness. And beneath that scrutiny, she felt herself wanting to be found worthy, though she didn't understand why.

"We need to leave," Marco urged, his voice tense. "Now."

But as they turned to go, their lights flickered and died, plunging them into absolute darkness. In that moment of blindness, Sophia felt something brush against her cheek—cold and smooth, like the scales of a serpent.

A voice whispered in her ear, in that same unknown language from her dream, but this time she understood perfectly: "You woke me for a reason. Now you must face what follows."

When their lights sputtered back to life, Dr. Thorn's face was pale. "We don't have much time," she said. "The binding is weakening. And she's choosing her targets."

"How do we stop it?" Elena asked, her voice barely audible.

Dr. Thorn's expression was grim. "I'm not sure we can. Or should. Some myths exist to be completed, not stopped."

Chapter 5
The Survivor

They returned to the surface in silence, each lost in their own thoughts about what Dr. Thorn had revealed. As they emerged from the cave, they found an unexpected visitor waiting—a young woman from the village, her eyes red from crying, her hands twisting nervously in the fabric of her dress.

"You are the archaeologists," she said in halting English. "The ones who opened the forbidden place."

Marco stepped forward. "Yes, we—"

"I need to tell you what I saw," the woman interrupted. "What happened to my mother and brother."

Her name was Athena—a cruel irony given the circumstances. She had been named for the goddess her family had traditionally revered. Now she spoke of that same goddess with fear and anger.

Inside Sophia's tent, Athena told her story between bouts of tears. Two nights earlier, her mother and brother had gone to leave offerings at a small shrine near the coast—a family tradition to ensure good fishing. They hadn't returned. Athena had gone looking for them the next morning.

"I found them on the path," she said, her voice breaking. "Like statues. Stone. But their faces..." She covered her own face with her hands. "They had seen something terrible. Something that—" She broke off, shuddering.

"Did you see anything else?" Sophia asked gently. "Anything unusual?"

Athena nodded slowly. "There was a mist, low to the ground. And I thought I saw a woman watching from the rocks. But when I looked directly, there was no one. Only..." She hesitated. "Only when I turned away, in the corner of my eye, I could see her again. Her hair... it moved like it was alive."

"But you saw her and weren't affected," Dr. Thorn noted. "Why do you think that is?"

Athena looked down at her hands. "I didn't look into her eyes. My grandmother told me the old stories—never look a Gorgon in the eyes. So I kept my gaze down. But I felt her watching me. And I heard—" She shook her head, as if trying to dislodge the memory.

"What did you hear?" Sophia pressed.

"A voice in my head. It said I was innocent. That I wasn't like the others."

Dr. Thorn and Sophia exchanged glances. "This suggests Medusa is making judgments," Dr. Thorn said. "She's not indiscriminately turning everyone to stone."

"Judgments based on what?" Marco asked.

"In the original myth, Medusa was a victim who was transformed into a weapon against men," Dr. Thorn explained. "But over time, that nuance was lost. She became simply a monster to be slain by the hero. Perhaps now she's reclaiming her narrative—punishing those she sees as complicit in systems of betrayal and injustice."

Sophia thought of the missing team members and villagers who had been transformed. "But Dr. Kalman, Mira—they had nothing to do with any injustice against Medusa. They were just scientists."

"Were they?" Dr. Thorn asked quietly. "Or were they, are we, disturbing a sacred space for our own glory? Taking artifacts, examining remains, all without true reverence for the history we claim to honor?"

The accusation hung in the air, uncomfortably close to truth. Sophia had pursued this excavation despite local warnings, driven by ambition and the desire to make her mark on the archaeological world.

"What's important now," Dr. Thorn continued, "is that Medusa's power seems to have evolved. In the original myth, her gaze turned men to stone immediately. Now, it seems she no longer requires direct eye contact. Recognition is enough—seeing her presence, even peripherally, while carrying something she judges as worthy of punishment."

"Emotional vulnerability," Sophia murmured, remembering the voice she had heard in the tomb. "She's looking into hearts, not just meeting eyes."

Athena, who had been listening intently, spoke up. "My grandmother said the Gorgon could see the truth behind all masks. That her real power wasn't in her gaze but in her ability to reflect back the true nature of those who looked upon her."

The mirror-shield fragments suddenly took on new significance. Perseus had used it not just to avoid direct eye contact but to avoid that deeper recognition—to shield himself from the truth of what he was doing.

"We need to understand what she wants," Sophia said decisively. "This isn't random violence. There's a pattern, a purpose."

"And if we understand it?" Marco asked. "What then?"

Sophia had no answer. But as the sun began to set, casting long shadows across the camp, she felt again that sense of being watched, evaluated. And deep within, a growing certainty that she was meant to be here, that her awakening of Medusa had been no accident but part of a design set in motion centuries ago.

That night, as the others slept fitfully, Sophia returned to the artifact container where they kept the fragments of the stone heart. In the dim light of her lamp, she carefully reassembled them like a three-dimensional puzzle.

As the final piece clicked into place, she felt a jolt of energy pass through her hands. The fissures between the fragments began to glow with a faint red light, pulsing slowly like a beating heart.

And in her mind, she heard that voice again: "Now you begin to understand. But there is more truth to uncover, and time grows short."

Chapter 6
Mirror of Self

Morning broke with news of more disappearances in the village. Fear had spread like contagion; many families had fled to the mainland, while others barricaded themselves in their homes, windows covered, doors sealed with ancient symbols of protection.

In the clear light of day, Sophia struggled to reconcile the scientific rationalist she had always been with the woman who had heard voices from a stone heart, who had glimpsed a mythological being at the edges of her vision. Dr. Thorn seemed to sense her inner conflict.

"The Ancient Greeks didn't draw the same hard lines between myth and reality that we do," she said as they shared a sparse breakfast. "Their myths were ways of understanding real events, real patterns in human experience. The gods were both metaphor and actual presence."

"That doesn't explain people turning to stone," Sophia countered.

Dr. Thorn shrugged. "Perhaps not literally. But consider—haven't you ever felt frozen by fear or shame? Haven't you ever felt someone's judgment harden you, change you irreversibly?"

Before Sophia could respond, Elena rushed into the tent, her face animated with discovery. "You need to see this," she said, holding out her tablet. "I've been analyzing the symbols around the mirror-shield pedestal, cross-referencing them with other artifacts from Gorgon cults. The shield wasn't just a weapon used against Medusa—it was originally a ritual object that belonged to her priestesses."

The tablet showed comparisons between the symbols in the tomb and those found on ancient ritual objects across the Mediterranean.

"The priestesses used the mirror in ceremonies of truth and judgment," Elena continued. "It was said to reveal the true nature of whoever gazed into it. Perseus corrupted its purpose, using it not to face truth but to avoid it."

"And now?" Marco asked.

"The fragments we found suggest it was deliberately broken after Perseus used it—to prevent further misuse. But it also means the shield's power was never properly contained." Elena scrolled to another image. "These inscriptions speak of Medusa's rage and sorrow permeating the shield, corrupting the ancient protective magic. After death, her essence fused with the mirror's power."

"Creating a new kind of curse," Sophia said slowly. "One that turns her story of victimization into a weapon against those she perceives as similar to her persecutors."

Dr. Thorn nodded grimly. "The texts suggest she began seeking out those who 'distort truth' and 'betray innocence'—kings who abused power, warriors who violated the innocent, priests who corrupted sacred trusts. The very people who would have justified Perseus's act as heroic."

"So she's been doing this throughout history?" Marco looked appalled. "Turning people to stone across centuries?"

"Not continuously," Dr. Thorn clarified. "The binding spell in the tomb was designed to contain her between cycles of activity. Something has always triggered her reawakening—typically disturbances to her resting place or attempts to use her remains for power."

Sophia thought of the stone heart, now fully reassembled and pulsing with that strange inner light. "We need to know more about who she really was—not just the myths, but the truth behind them."

They spent the day poring over the imagery in the tomb, with Dr. Thorn translating the oldest inscriptions. What emerged was a narrative far different from the classical myth—Medusa had been not just a priestess but a oracle, blessed with the ability to see hidden truths. Her transformation had been a perversion of this gift, turning insight into a weapon.

"Athena's 'blessing' was a curse disguised as protection," Dr. Thorn explained, tracing the sequence of images that showed Medusa's transformation. "By making her gaze lethal, she ensured Medusa could never again be part of human society. The snakes were not just a mark of monstrosity but symbols of wisdom and foresight corrupted into instruments of fear."

"So Medusa was a victim turned into a weapon," Sophia said. "Used by the gods in their power struggles, then villainized to justify her murder."

"And now her rage has outlived her," Elena added softly. "Seeking justice or perhaps just recognition of what was done to her."

As evening approached, they prepared to return to the tomb. Sophia felt drawn there, compelled by something beyond scholarly curiosity. But as they gathered their equipment, Marco called out in alarm from the perimeter of the camp.

A strange mist had begun to swirl among the olive trees, too dense and purposeful to be natural. Within it, they glimpsed that now-familiar silhouette—a woman's form with writhing serpentine hair.

"Don't look directly at her!" Dr. Thorn shouted, but her warning came too late for Elena, who had turned instinctively toward the movement.

Their colleague froze, her expression shifting from curiosity to horror as she beheld something the others couldn't see. Then, with terrible swiftness, the transformation took her—skin, clothes, equipment all transmuting into the same gray stone as the other victims.

"Inside, now!" Sophia grabbed Marco and Dr. Thorn, pulling them into the nearest tent. They huddled there in the growing darkness, listening to the unnatural silence outside.

"She's getting closer," Marco whispered. "More powerful. We need to leave this island."

But Dr. Thorn shook her head. "Running won't help. She's awakened now, and her influence will spread. The only way forward is through the ritual suggested by the tomb inscriptions—someone must face her, acknowledge her truth, and either bind her again or release her from the cycle."

"Release her?" Marco looked incredulous. "You want to free a vengeful Gorgon to roam the world?"

"Not exactly," Dr. Thorn said. "The inscriptions suggest a third possibility—integration. Acceptance of her story, her power, her purpose. Not as a monster, but as a force of justice that has been twisted by centuries of misunderstanding."

Outside, the mist thickened. Through the tent walls, they could see the silhouette moving closer, circling them like a predator assessing its prey.

"She's choosing," Dr. Thorn whispered. "Deciding which of us is worthy to face her."

In that moment, Sophia felt a profound certainty that she would be the one chosen—that she had been marked from the moment she first touched the fragments of the stone heart. The voice she had heard, the connection she had felt—it had all been leading to this moment.

"I'll do it," she said, her voice steadier than she felt. "I'll perform the ritual. I'll face her."

Dr. Thorn looked at her intently. "Are you certain? This isn't just about courage. It's about truth—your truth. She will see everything—every lie, every betrayal, every self-deception."

Sophia thought of her career built on ambition, of relationships sacrificed for professional advancement, of ethical corners cut in the name of discovery. And deeper still, a personal connection to this place she hadn't yet acknowledged even to herself.

"I'm certain," she said. "I need to do this."

As the words left her lips, the silhouette outside became still. The mist retreated slightly, as if in acknowledgment of her decision.

Dr. Thorn nodded solemnly. "Then we prepare. The ritual must be performed at dawn, in the chamber where her heart was kept. And you must go alone."

Chapter 7
Stone Garden

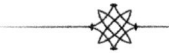

They spent the night preparing for the ritual, with Dr. Thorn coaching Sophia on the ancient words and gestures described in the tomb inscriptions. Marco remained skeptical, vacillating between fear for their safety and reluctant fascination with the unfolding events.

"Even if this is real," he argued, "even if Medusa's essence has somehow survived and is now active, why you? Why are you the one who has to face her?"

Sophia hesitated, then reached into her field journal and removed a faded photograph. It showed a younger version of herself alongside a tall, bearded man in archaeological gear, both smiling in front of a different Greek ruin.

"My father," she explained. "Dr. Alexander Hass. He disappeared during an expedition to these islands fifteen years ago. The official report said he was lost at sea during a storm, but..." She shook her head. "He was obsessed with the Gorgon myths, convinced they concealed the location of an ancient temple with unimaginable artifacts. The night before he disappeared, he called me, more excited than I'd ever heard him. He said he'd found something remarkable in a cave on Kythinos."

Understanding dawned on Marco's face. "You weren't randomly assigned to this dig. You requested it."

"I pulled every string, called in every favor," Sophia admitted. "I've spent my entire career building the credentials that would give me access to this site. Not just for the archaeology but to find out what happened to him."

Dr. Thorn studied Sophia with new interest. "The personal connection matters. Medusa responds to emotional truth, to genuine seeking. Your father may have awakened her before, begun the process that you've now completed."

Before dawn, they made their way back to the cave entrance. The island was eerily quiet, as if all natural life had retreated in the face of the ancient power that had been unleashed. Even the sea seemed to hold its breath, its waves subdued against the shore.

At the entrance to the tomb, Dr. Thorn embraced Sophia briefly. "Remember, the mirror fragments are key. They were broken to prevent misuse, but in the ritual, they can be briefly reunited in purpose if not in form. Use them to reflect both her truth and yours."

Marco handed her a small pack containing the ritual items they had prepared. "I still think this is insane," he said, but his voice held resignation rather than judgment. "Just... come back, okay?"

Sophia descended alone into the tomb, her headlamp casting strange shadows on the ancient frescos. As she reached the main chamber, she found it transformed. The air was thick with that strange mist, and the stone floor was now covered in a mosaic of reflective fragments, as if the mirror-shield had multiplied its broken pieces across the entire space.

But more disturbing was what lay beyond the central pedestal—a garden of stone figures, dozens of them, arranged in concentric circles around the alcove where the heart had been kept. Each was frozen in a moment of terror or revelation, their features preserved in perfect, horrifying detail.

They weren't random victims, Sophia realized as she moved among them. Their clothing and adornments spanned different eras—ancient priests in ceremonial garb, medieval knights, renaissance nobles, Victorian gentlemen, modern figures in business suits and military uniforms. All of them men of power and authority. All of them caught in that moment of recognition when they saw their true nature reflected back at them.

And then, at the center of this grim collection, she found what she had unconsciously been seeking all these years—a figure she recognized despite the stone transformation. Her father, his face locked in an expression not of fear but of wonder, his hand outstretched as if reaching for something just beyond his grasp.

"Dad," she whispered, touching his cold stone face. "What did you find here? What did you see?"

The mist thickened around her, coalescing into tendrils that caressed her face like curious fingers. That voice she had heard before whispered in her mind: "He saw truth. He recognized me. But he came as a taker, not a seeker. His wonder was for glory, not understanding."

Sophia turned slowly, knowing what she would see. In the center of the chamber stood Medusa—not the monstrous figure of myth but a woman of unearthly beauty, her features both ancient and timeless. Only her hair betrayed her inhuman nature—a writhing mass of serpents that hissed and coiled around her face like a living crown. Her eyes were closed, but Sophia could feel the weight of her attention nonetheless.

"I've come to understand," Sophia said, her voice echoing in the chamber. "To see your truth."

The figure inclined her head slightly. "Many have claimed to seek understanding. Few have been willing to face the cost of true seeing."

"I'm ready," Sophia said, reaching for the reassembled stone heart in her pack. "Show me what I need to see."

Medusa moved closer, her movement unnaturally fluid, as if she were floating rather than walking. The serpents of her hair extended toward Sophia, their forked tongues flicking at the air around her face.

"Your father sought knowledge without wisdom," Medusa said, her voice resonating directly in Sophia's mind rather than through the air. "He sought power without understanding its price. Like so many before him, he looked but did not see."

Images flooded Sophia's consciousness—her father discovering the tomb, his excitement not at the historical significance but at the potential fame, the academic recognition, the chance to prove his theories right. She saw him reaching for the stone heart, felt his dismay when it crumbled at his touch, sensed his terror when the mist began to form around him.

"You are his blood," Medusa continued. "But are you his mirror? Do you seek for the same reasons? Will you use what you find for the same purposes?"

The truth burned in Sophia's chest. Yes, she had come seeking answers about her father, but hadn't she also been driven by the same ambition? The same desire to make her mark, to uncover secrets others couldn't, to claim discovery?

"I don't know," she admitted, both to Medusa and to herself. "I want to believe I'm different, but I'm not sure I am."

The honesty of this admission seemed to please Medusa. The serpents of her hair relaxed slightly, their movements becoming less agitated.

"Then perhaps there is hope for you yet," she said. "The ritual awaits. Will you proceed?"

Sophia nodded and began to arrange the mirror fragments in the pattern Dr. Thorn had described—a spiraling circle around the reassembled heart. As she worked, she felt the weight of centuries pressing down on her, as if time itself were condensing in this ancient chamber.

Chapter 8
The Rebirth

The ritual began with the ancient words Dr. Thorn had taught her—a language older than classical Greek, its syllables rough and primal in Sophia's mouth. As she spoke, the fragments of the mirror-shield began to glow with an inner light, reflecting not the chamber around them but scenes from Medusa's life—her time as a priestess, her violation, her transformation, her exile, her death.

Medusa herself remained still, her eyes closed, but her presence seemed to expand with each word Sophia uttered, filling the chamber with a palpable energy. The serpents of her hair grew more animated, their bodies elongating and thickening, their scales catching the strange light from the mirrors.

When the final word of the incantation faded, Medusa opened her eyes.

Sophia had braced herself for the legendary lethal gaze, but what she saw was more complex and more terrible than simple death. Medusa's eyes held no pupils, no irises—only reflective surfaces like living mercury that showed Sophia herself, but not as she was. The reflection showed all her possibilities—the scholar she had aspired to be, the ruthless careerist she sometimes was, the frightened daughter still seeking her father's approval, the woman capable of both great insight and deliberate blindness.

"Now you begin to see," Medusa said, her voice louder now, resonating through the chamber. "Not just me, but yourself. The mirror works both ways."

The serpents of her hair had become fully animated now, their bodies thick as Sophia's arm, their movements hypnotic and deliberate. They stretched toward her, not threatening but curious, tasting the air around her with flickering tongues.

"You are neither innocent nor guilty," Medusa continued. "Like all humans, you contain both truth and deception, both the capacity to see and the desire to look away."

She moved closer, inhumanly beautiful and monstrous all at once. Her skin had a translucent quality that revealed glimpses of the structures beneath—not blood and bone but crystalline formations that caught and refracted light.

"What do you want?" Sophia asked, fighting the urge to step back. "Why have you returned now?"

Instead of answering directly, Medusa raised her arms. The mist that had filled the chamber swirled more intensely, forming images—visions of the modern world with all its chaos and cruelty, its technological wonders and moral failures.

"I have watched from the shadows for centuries," Medusa said. "Seen the rise and fall of empires, philosophies, religions. Seen how little humans have changed beneath their evolving costumes. The same patterns repeat—the powerful prey upon the vulnerable, then rewrite history to cast themselves as heroes."

The visions shifted to show moments throughout history—conquerors standing over fallen cities, priests condemning the innocent, leaders inciting hatred for their own gain. Then more intimate scenes—domestic violence hidden behind respectable facades, powerful men abusing their positions, victims silenced by shame or fear.

"The Gorgon was never meant to be a monster," Medusa said. "But a mirror—reflecting the true monstrosity of those who looked upon her. Perseus didn't slay a beast; he shattered the mirror that would have shown him his own nature."

"And now?" Sophia asked, her voice barely audible over the hissing of the serpents.

"Now I seek more than vengeance," Medusa replied. "I seek a legacy. The world has forgotten what I truly was—has accepted the hero's version of the story for too long."

She gestured at the stone figures surrounding them. "These men saw the truth at the end, but too late for it to matter. Their recognition changed nothing. I need someone who can carry my truth back into the world, who can ensure the story is finally told correctly."

The implication hung in the air between them. Medusa wasn't just seeking justice or revenge—she was looking for a successor, a witness, an apostle.

"Why me?" Sophia asked, though she was beginning to understand.

"Because you woke me," Medusa said simply. "Because you sought truth, even if for imperfect reasons. Because you have the knowledge to understand what I was and what I became. And because—" She reached out, one pale finger almost touching Sophia's cheek. "Because you know what it is to be overlooked, to have your voice dismissed, to be valued only for what you can provide rather than who you are."

The insight struck uncomfortably close to home. Throughout her academic career, Sophia had fought to be taken seriously, had worked twice as hard for half the recognition, had watched less qualified men claim credit for discoveries she had made.

"What would carrying your legacy mean?" she asked carefully.

Medusa smiled, a surprisingly human expression on her otherworldly face. "That is for the ritual to reveal. The choice, when it comes, will be yours."

As if responding to an unseen signal, the serpents of Medusa's hair extended fully, surrounding Sophia in a living circle of scaled bodies. The reassembled stone heart began to pulse more rapidly, its light turning from red to a deep purple.

"The next phase begins," Medusa said. "Prepare yourself. The reflection ritual demands absolute truth—from both of us."

Chapter 9
The Reflection Ritual

The serpents surrounding Sophia began to move in unison, creating a rhythmic pattern that matched the pulsing of the stone heart. The mirror fragments lifted from the ground, suspended in the air, their surfaces now swirling with images too rapid to distinguish.

"The reflection ritual has been performed only rarely throughout history," Medusa explained, her voice taking on a ceremonial cadence. "It requires one who can face the Gorgon's truth without turning away, without the shield of self-deception."

The suspended mirrors began to orbit around them, picking up speed until they formed a glittering, fragmented sphere of light. Within this sphere, past and present seemed to merge—the ancient chamber transforming momentarily into Athena's temple as it had been millennia ago, then back again.

"The ritual has three phases," Medusa continued. "First, you must witness my truth—not the myth, but what actually happened."

The mirrors flashed, and suddenly Sophia was no longer merely watching but experiencing Medusa's memories as if they were her own. She felt the pride of being chosen as Athena's priestess, the sacred responsibility of maintaining the temple, the devotion to a goddess who promised wisdom and protection. Then came the violation—Poseidon's violence and entitlement, the helpless rage, the desperate prayers to Athena for intervention that went unanswered until it was too late.

The transformation came next—not a blessing but an agonizing metamorphosis as human flesh gave way to something other, as her hair writhed into serpents, as her eyes became weapons that reflected back the horror of what had been done to her. She experienced Medusa's exile, the decades of solitude, the gradual hardening of sorrow into rage, of victimhood into a terrible power.

Finally, Perseus—not the noble hero of myth but a youth manipulated by power-hungry kings, armed with divine weapons, and sent to murder a woman whose only crime had been surviving her own destruction. She felt the sword at her neck, the final indignity of her head taken as a trophy, her power harvested as a weapon.

When the vision faded, Sophia found herself on her knees, tears streaming down her face. "They rewrote you," she whispered. "They turned the victim into the villain."

"As happens so often," Medusa acknowledged. "History belongs to those who survive to tell it—usually those who hold power."

The mirrors shifted again, glowing more intensely. "The second phase requires you to witness your own truth—to see yourself as clearly as you have seen me."

This vision was even more difficult to bear. Sophia watched her life unfold with merciless clarity—her childhood seeking approval from a father who valued discovery over family, her determination to follow in his footsteps despite the cost, her willingness to exploit archaeological sites and cultural heritage for academic advancement. She saw relationships abandoned when they became inconvenient, ethical compromises justified in the name of research, the slow corruption of genuine curiosity into ambition and ego.

But she also saw moments of genuine insight, of compassion, of growth. She saw her capacity for wonder, for reverence, for recognition of something greater than herself. She saw her potential to become either like her father—brilliant but ultimately destructive—or something better.

When this vision ended, Sophia remained silent, humbled by the unvarnished truth of her own nature.

"Few can bear to see themselves so clearly," Medusa said, her voice gentler now. "Most prefer the comfortable lies they tell themselves."

"What is the third phase?" Sophia asked, her voice raw from crying.

"The third phase is choice," Medusa answered. "Now that you have witnessed both truths, you must decide what follows. The ritual offers three possibilities."

She gestured, and three of the mirror fragments enlarged, floating before Sophia.

"The first is binding," Medusa explained. "You can restore the ancient containment, return me to slumber, and leave this island with your knowledge. The cycle would continue, and someday another would awaken me again."

The first mirror showed an image of the tomb resealed, the stone heart once again broken and contained.

"The second is banishment," she continued. "You can use the ritual to sever my connection to this world entirely. My essence would be scattered beyond recall, my power ended. The petrifications would cease, but so would any chance of my story being truly known."

The second mirror displayed a vision of the tomb empty, the stone figures returning to flesh, Medusa's presence fading like mist in sunlight.

"And the third?" Sophia asked, though she suspected she already knew.

"The third is integration," Medusa said. "Not possession, not domination, but partnership. You would carry a portion of my essence, become a modern vessel for an ancient power. Through you, I could finally tell my story in my own words. Through me, you would gain the ability to see truth behind all masks, to reflect back the true nature of those who would deceive or harm."

The third mirror showed Sophia leaving the island transformed—outwardly the same but her eyes occasionally flashing with that same mercurial reflection, her shadow sometimes suggesting serpentine movement.

"There is risk in this third path," Medusa warned. "My power is not easily contained in human form. My rage has simmered for millennia. You would have to learn to control it, to channel it justly. And the world would eventually recognize what you carry—some would fear you, others seek to destroy you."

Sophia stared at the three choices floating before her. "Is there no other way? No path that allows both justice for you and peace?"

"Justice and peace rarely walk hand in hand," Medusa said sadly. "But perhaps, over time, they might learn to do so through you. The choice, however, must be yours."

The chamber fell silent except for the soft hissing of the serpents and the humming energy of the mirror fragments. Sophia closed her eyes, weighing not just her future but the weight of an ancient wrong that had reverberated through centuries.

"Before I choose," she said finally, "I need to know one thing. If I choose integration, what happens to those already turned to stone? My father, the villagers, my colleagues?"

Medusa's expression was unreadable. "Their fate is fixed. The petrification cannot be undone—it is a physical transformation, not merely an enchantment. They saw truth too late and could not bear it. But you could prevent others from sharing their fate."

Sophia looked at her father's stone figure, forever frozen in that moment of revelation. There would be no reunion, no closure beyond this recognition of his end. The grief of that finality washed through her, along with the understanding that her quest had always been destined to end this way.

"I need to perform the ritual correctly," she said, her decision made but not yet voiced. "I'm ready for the final phase."

Chapter 10
Gaze of the Damned

The mirrors began to spin faster, their light intensifying until the chamber was filled with fractured reflections. Medusa instructed Sophia to stand at the center of the circle, directly across from her, with the reassembled stone heart between them.

"For the ritual to be completed properly, you will need assistance," Medusa said. "Someone to witness your choice, to ground the ritual in the present world."

Before Sophia could ask how this would be possible when she had come alone, the mist swirled at the chamber entrance. Marco emerged, his expression dazed but determined.

"I couldn't let you face this alone," he said, moving to stand beside her. "Dr. Thorn said I might be needed."

Sophia felt a surge of gratitude at his presence, but also concern. "You shouldn't be here. It's dangerous."

"Life is dangerous," he replied with a faint smile. "Besides, what kind of assistant would I be if I abandoned you at the crucial moment?"

Medusa observed their exchange with those mirror-like eyes that revealed nothing of her thoughts. "He has come of his own will," she said. "That matters. The ritual requires willing participation."

She instructed Marco to stand at the third point of a triangle, completing the geometry of the ritual. The mirrors adjusted their orbit to encompass all three figures.

"Now," Medusa said, "the final words must be spoken, and the choice made manifest. Each participant must speak their truth—no lies, no evasions. Only absolute honesty will complete the ritual."

Marco was to speak first. He stood tall in the swirling light, his face reflecting determination despite the fear evident in his eyes.

"I am Marco Diaz," he began, his voice gaining strength as he spoke. "I came to this expedition seeking adventure and advancement. I've followed Dr. Hass because I admire her work and hoped some of her prestige would elevate my own career."

So far, his words rang true. But as he continued, something in his voice changed subtly.

"I believe in science and rationality. I reject these superstitions about curses and ancient powers. This ritual is merely a psychological experience, nothing more."

The moment the falsehood left his lips, the mirrors shuddered. The serpents surrounding them hissed in agitation. Medusa's expression shifted from neutral to sorrowful.

"He lies," she said simply. "He speaks what he thinks should be true, not what he knows in his heart."

Marco's eyes widened as the mist began to swirl around him, thickening into tendrils that coiled around his legs. "No, I—" He looked at Sophia, panic rising in his face. "I do believe it! I have to believe it, or else everything I understand about the world is wrong!"

"The ritual demands truth," Medusa repeated. "Not what you wish to believe, but what you know."

He struggled against the encroaching mist, but it continued to climb up his body. "Sophia, help me!"

Sophia reached for him, but Medusa raised a hand to stop her. "You cannot intervene. The ritual has its own rules, its own justice. If he cannot speak truth, he cannot participate."

"Marco," Sophia urged, "just say what you really feel, what you really believe!"

His eyes met hers, filled with terror and resignation. "I believe," he whispered, his voice breaking. "I've seen too much not to believe. But I'm afraid of what it means—that the world isn't what I thought, that there are powers beyond our understanding, that everything I've built my identity around might be wrong."

For a moment, it seemed his confession might be enough. The mist paused in its advance. But then he added, "But I still think we should destroy this place, bury these artifacts, and never speak of what happened here. Some knowledge is too dangerous."

The final calculation—the prioritizing of safety over truth—was his undoing. The mist surged upward, enveloping him completely. When it receded, Marco stood transformed into stone, his face frozen in a moment of terrible realization.

"No!" Sophia cried, reaching toward the stone figure that had been her colleague and friend.

"He chose fear over truth at the final moment," Medusa said, her voice heavy with what might have been regret. "As so many do. He could not bear to fully face what he had discovered."

Grief and anger surged through Sophia. "You didn't have to do that! He was trying!"

"I did not transform him," Medusa corrected gently. "The ritual did. Or rather, his own inability to fully embrace truth did. The Gorgon's gaze only reveals what is already there—the capacity for self-deception, the preference for comfortable lies."

Sophia stared at Marco's stone figure, her mind racing. She had brought him into this. His fate was on her hands.

"The ritual continues," Medusa said. "Now you must speak your truth, Sophia Hass. And then make your choice."

Sophia stood in the center of the swirling mirrors, the stone heart pulsing between her and Medusa. The wrongness of Marco's fate crystallized something within her—a determination that no one else would suffer if she could prevent it.

"I am Sophia Hass," she began, her voice quiet but steady. "I came here seeking answers about my father, but also seeking professional recognition. I ignored warnings, disrespected local traditions, and disturbed what should have been left in peace."

The mirrors hummed in response to her honesty, their light warming from cool blue to a softer gold.

"I've spent my life pursuing knowledge, but not always wisdom. I've used people. I've cut corners. I've told myself that discovery justifies almost any means."

She looked at her father's stone figure, then at Marco's. "I've caused harm through my ambition and my blindness. And now others have paid the price for my choices."

Tears streamed down her face, but she continued, laying bare every secret she had kept even from herself—her jealousy of more successful colleagues, her occasional falsification of data to support theories, her use of her father's reputation to advance her own career while privately resenting his abandonment.

When she finally fell silent, emotionally exhausted, the mirrors had turned a deep amber color, their movement slowing.

"You have spoken true," Medusa acknowledged. "Few have the courage to see themselves so clearly. Now comes the choice—

binding, banishment, or integration. What will you choose, Sophia Hass?"

Sophia looked at the three mirrors still floating before her, each showing a possible future. The first two offered a return to normalcy, to the world as she had known it—either with Medusa contained and waiting for the next awakening, or with her essence scattered beyond recall.

But it was the third option that called to her—not just for herself, but for the truth it would allow to be told.

"Integration," she said firmly. "I choose to carry your truth into the world."

The moment the words left her lips, the stone heart between them cracked open. Inside was not stone but crystalline flesh, still somehow beating after millennia. Medusa reached down and lifted it, holding it cupped in her palms.

"Are you certain?" she asked one final time. "This cannot be undone. You will never again be only yourself."

Sophia thought of all she would be giving up—the simplicity of a singular identity, the comfort of not knowing the depths of others' souls, the privilege of looking away from uncomfortable truths. But she also thought of what might be gained—not just for herself, but for all those whose stories had been rewritten by the powerful, whose sufferings had been justified or erased.

"I'm certain," she said. "Let it be done."

Medusa nodded solemnly. "Then come. Look into my eyes without fear, and accept what I have to give."

Sophia stepped forward, her gaze meeting Medusa's fully for the first time. In those mercurial depths, she saw not death but a terrible, beautiful clarity—the world as it truly was, stripped of all illusion and comfort.

Medusa lifted the beating crystal heart between them. It pulsed with power, shedding droplets of a fluid that was neither blood nor water but something older than both. She pressed it against Sophia's chest, directly over her human heart.

The pain was immediate and overwhelming—not just physical but existential, as if her very being were being rewritten on a cellular level. She felt Medusa's consciousness flowing into her like a river of ancient memory, carrying with it rage and sorrow and wisdom beyond human comprehension.

She screamed, the sound echoing through the chamber and beyond, out into the world that would soon know her—and through her, know Medusa—in a new way.

The mirror fragments spun faster, then shattered into thousands of tiny shards that embedded themselves in the stone walls of the chamber, each one catching and holding a fragment of the ritual's light.

As Sophia collapsed to her knees, she felt the transformation taking hold—not an outside change, but something internal and profound. Her vision fragmented briefly, showing her not just the physical world but the truths that lay beneath appearances— the hidden motives, the secret shames, the authentic selves people concealed even from themselves.

When she finally rose, she was both Sophia and not-Sophia— still herself, but carrying within her something ancient and powerful that had waited millennia for this moment of rebirth.

Medusa stood before her, her form already beginning to fade. "It is done," she said, her voice now audible within Sophia's mind as well as without. "I have given you what remains of my essence. Use it wisely, see clearly, judge justly."

"Will you... are you gone?" Sophia asked, reaching toward the diminishing figure.

"Not gone," Medusa's voice replied as her visible form dissipated into mist. "Transformed. Integrated. Part of you now, as you are part of me. The Gorgon lives on, but with a new purpose, a new vessel, a new chance to be understood."

The mist swirled one last time around Sophia, then settled onto her skin like dew, absorbed into her being. The chamber fell silent, the ritual complete.

Sophia stood alone among the stone figures, her father and Marco among them, permanent witnesses to what had transpired. She felt different—her senses sharper, her awareness expanded. And deep within, she felt Medusa's presence—not controlling, not dominating, but integrated into her consciousness like a new dimension of perception.

When she finally ascended from the tomb, Dr. Thorn was waiting, her face anxious in the dawn light.

"It's done," Sophia said simply. "She's part of me now."

Dr. Thorn studied her face intently. "Your eyes," she whispered. "They've changed."

Sophia knew without seeing that her irises now held that same mercurial quality—not always visible, but present when she chose to truly see, to recognize the truth behind appearances.

"Marco?" Dr. Thorn asked, looking past her toward the cave entrance.

Sophia shook her head sadly. "He couldn't embrace the full truth. He's with the others now. Part of her garden of stone."

As they walked back toward the camp, Dr. Thorn asked the question Sophia had been asking herself: "What will you do now?"

Chapter 11
Legacy of the Gorgon

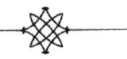

Three months after the events on Kythinos, Sophia Hass stood before an audience at the International Archaeological Congress in Athens. Her paper, "Reexamining the Gorgon Mythos: Archaeological Evidence for Historical Revision," had drawn an overflow crowd of academics, journalists, and curious listeners.

Her appearance had changed subtly since the island. Her hair, once straight and practical, now fell in thick waves that seemed to move slightly even in still air. Her eyes, normally a warm brown, occasionally caught the light in ways that made observers uneasy, reflecting back something more than mere physical presence.

But the most profound changes were invisible to casual observation. She saw the world differently now—people's words overlaid with their true intentions, social masks transparent to her heightened perception. The Medusa-consciousness within her provided context for what she observed, an ancient wisdom that helped her navigate the complexities of modern human interactions.

"The traditional narrative of Medusa as monster and Perseus as hero represents a deliberate political revision," she explained to the rapt audience. "Archaeological evidence from the recently discovered temple on Kythinos suggests a different story—one of a respected oracle transformed against her will, then villainized to justify her murder."

On the screen behind her, images of the tomb appeared—the frescos showing Medusa's transformation, the ritual chamber, the fragments of the mirror-shield. Notably absent were photos of the stone figures or the heart. Those secrets she kept, protecting both the dead and the living from truths they weren't prepared to face.

As she spoke, she felt that familiar presence within her—not separate from her consciousness but interwoven with it, offering insights, suggesting connections, occasionally urging caution when she strayed too close to revealing too much.

The integration hadn't been easy. There had been moments in those first weeks when Medusa's rage had threatened to overwhelm her, when the temptation to use her new power against those who deserved judgment had been almost irresistible. She had seen colleagues who built careers on stolen ideas, administrators who abused their positions, men whose behavior toward women echoed Poseidon's ancient entitlement.

But she had made a promise—to use the power justly, to be a witness to truth rather than an executioner. She had learned to channel Medusa's essence into her work instead, into a scholarly revolution that challenged centuries of accepted mythology.

After her presentation, a senior professor approached her, his expression caught between admiration and suspicion. "Fascinating theory, Dr. Hass," he said, his smile not reaching his eyes. "But rather speculative, wouldn't you say? These interpretations of the imagery seem... personally motivated rather than objectively derived."

Sophia met his gaze directly, allowing just a flicker of her true perception to surface. In that moment of connection, he saw himself reflected back—not as the respected scholar he presented to the world, but as the intellectual bully who suppressed competing theories and claimed credit for his students' work.

He stepped back involuntarily, a flash of fear crossing his face. "Your eyes," he muttered. "For a moment, I thought..." He didn't finish the sentence, turning abruptly and disappearing into the crowd.

Dr. Thorn, who had witnessed the exchange, moved to Sophia's side. "You need to be more careful," she warned quietly. "That was dangerously close to revelation."

"He needed to see himself clearly," Sophia replied. "Just for a moment."

"And if he had been turned to stone in the middle of an archaeological conference?"

Sophia shook her head. "That's not how it works now. The integration changed the nature of the power. I don't petrify with a glance—I reflect truth. What people do with that truth is their choice."

Nevertheless, she knew Dr. Thorn was right about caution. The world wasn't ready to know about what had happened on Kythinos, about what she now carried within her. For now, her mission was more subtle—to rewrite the academic understanding of the Gorgon myths, to restore Medusa's true story to the historical record, and to use her unique perception to identify those whose modern myths needed similar revision.

The stone figures remained in the tomb, which had been officially sealed as a protected archaeological site, with access restricted to a select few researchers under Sophia's supervision. Her father and Marco were listed among those lost during the excavation, their bodies never recovered. It was a lie, but a necessary one.

Sometimes at night, especially when the moon was full, Sophia would feel Medusa's consciousness becoming more active within her, sharing memories of ancient times, of a world where gods walked among humans and monsters were often those with the most power, not the most visible differences from the norm.

These communions left her with a deeper understanding of her responsibility. She was not just an archaeologist now, nor merely the vessel for an ancient power. She was the bridge between myth and truth, between past injustice and future recognition.

Six months after the conference, Sophia stood in her bathroom, examining her reflection in the mirror. For just a moment, her hair seemed to move with a life of its own, coiling and uncoiling like drowsy serpents. Her eyes flashed silver, reflecting back not just her physical appearance but the complex truth of what she had become.

"We are changing," she whispered to her reflection. "Both of us."

The integration was becoming more complete with each passing day. Medusa's rage was softening through exposure to modern life, to experiences her ancient consciousness had never known. And Sophia found herself adopting aspects of Medusa's perspective—her unflinching assessment of human nature, her refusal to accept comfortable lies, her capacity to see beauty in what others called monstrous.

She had begun writing a book—not just an academic text, but a retelling of Medusa's story from the inside, framed as fiction but containing the emotional truth of what had happened millennia ago. It would be her way of fulfilling her promise to carry Medusa's truth into the world, to ensure her story was finally told correctly.

As she prepared for bed that night, Sophia noticed a small envelope that had been slipped under her apartment door. Inside was a single photograph—a shot of her speaking at the conference, caught at a moment when her eyes had flashed that telltale silver, when her hair had seemed to move independently.

On the back, someone had written: "I know what you are. We should talk."

The note was signed with a symbol Sophia recognized from her studies—the ancient mark of Athena's priestesses, those who had first contained Medusa's essence after her death. Those who had created the binding spell and the ritual that had ultimately led to her integration.

They were still out there, then—the keepers of the old knowledge, the watchers of boundaries between myth and reality. And they had recognized what she carried.

Sophia placed the photo on her nightstand, unafraid. Let them come. Let them see what she and Medusa had become together. Let them witness the new Gorgon—not a monster to be slain, not a victim to be pitied, but a force for truth in a world built on comfortable lies.

She felt Medusa's consciousness stir within her, curious about this development. The serpentine presence that had once been foreign now felt as natural as her own thoughts, a partner rather than a passenger.

"They're watching us," she said to the presence within her.

Let them watch, came the response, heard not with ears but with some deeper sense. *Let them see. The truth cannot remain in shadow forever.*

Sophia smiled as she turned out the light. In the darkness, her eyes glowed briefly with that silvery light—the Gorgon's gaze, now turned toward a future where ancient wrongs might finally be acknowledged, where myths might be rewritten to reveal rather than conceal truth.

The curse lived on, but transformed—no longer a weapon of indiscriminate petrification, but a gift of clarity, of recognition, of reflection. As Sophia drifted toward sleep, she felt Medusa's consciousness merging more completely with her own, a union of modern scholarship and ancient power, of human compassion and inhuman perception.

Together, they would rewrite the story. Together, they would ensure that those who looked upon them would see not a monster, but a mirror.

THE END

Enjoyed this book?

Share your thoughts with a review and help more readers discover it! Your feedback truly makes a difference.

☆☆☆☆☆

To be the first to read my next book or for any suggestions about new translations, visit: https://arielsandersbooks.com/

SPECIAL BONUS
Want this Bonus Ebook for *free*?

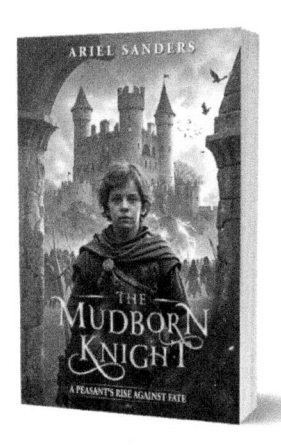

SCAN W/ YOUR CAMERA TO DOWNLOAD THE EBOOK!

SCAN ME

Printed in Dunstable, United Kingdom